This igloo book belongs to:

....

Contents

igloobooks

Published in 2019
by Igloo Books Ltd
Cottage Farm
Sywell
NN6 0BJ
www.igloobooks.com

1019 001
2 4 6 8 10 9 7 5 3 1
ISBN 978-1-78810-593-4

Illustrated by Mike Garton
Written by Melanie Joyce

Printed and manufactured in China

Stories for  Year Olds

igloobooks

Carrie the Climber

Carrie's brother, Ben, had climbed up to the tree house in their garden. "I want to climb up, too," said Carrie. But Ben pulled up the ladder and said, "No, Carrie, you can't come up."

"You're too small to climb the ladder," said Dad. "It's a little bit too high," said Mum. But Carrie was determined to climb up to the tree house.

So, when no one was looking, Carrie went to the shed and pulled out her play chair and her plastic toy box. "I'll be big enough to climb up now," she said.

Carrie climbed onto the box and then onto the chair.
"I'm nearly there," she said and she gave a little kick.
But the chair slipped and fell with a *thunk,* onto the grass.
"Help!" cried Carrie. "I'm stuck!"

Ben looked down and Mum looked up. Then, Dad ran as fast as he could to the bottom of the tree. He reached up to Carrie and said, "Hold on to me." Soon, Carrie was safe and sound, back on the ground.

8

"It is important to listen to what we say," said Mum.
"Sorry, Mum," said Carrie. "But one day, I'm going to
be a very good tree climber."
Everyone smiled. "We know you will," they said.

9

Bonny's Dolly

Bonny had lost her best dolly on holiday. When she came home, she played with Teddy and she played with Bunny, but it wasn't the same. "I want my best dolly!" cried Bonny.

Mum gave Bonny a lovely soft cuddle. "Would you like to go next door and play with Cilla?" she asked. "That will cheer you up."

"Yes, please," said Bonny and she wiped away her tears.

At Cilla's house, Bonny did some drawing and played on the swing. Then, Cilla's mum brought out the toy box. It was full of lovely toys.

"Look, here's my best dolly," said Cilla with a great big smile. But poor Bonny didn't have a best dolly to play with anymore and she began to cry.

"Don't worry, Bonny," said Cilla's mummy, gently.
"There are lots of pretty dollies here to play with." She got
them out of the toy box. "Pick the one you like the most,"
she said.

Bonny had a lovely time playing with the dollies. Cilla and her mummy were very kind because they let Bonny keep the one she liked the best. "Thank you," said Bonny. She was very happy. It felt lovely to have a new best dolly.

Well Done, Leonard

A stranger had come to live at Leonard's house. Mum said it was Leonard's baby brother and he was called Charlie. Dad said that Leonard was a big brother now and it was a very important job.

But Leonard didn't like being a big brother.
Charlie couldn't talk or run about, or play in the garden.
In fact, he spent most of the time asleep. "Being a big
brother is boring," said Leonard.

One day, Mum was busy cleaning. The vacuum cleaner whirred and crackled and made a terrible racket. Charlie woke up and began to cry. Mum couldn't hear and Dad couldn't hear. But Leonard could hear.

He ran into the living room and tugged at Mum's arm.
"Charlie's crying," he said.
So, Mum went to give Charlie a cuddle. "Well done,
Leonard," she said.
"Well done," said Dad. "You're a very good big brother."

As a special treat, Mum and Dad took Leonard to
the park. He slid down the slide and whirled around
on the roundabout.

"I can't wait for Charlie to be old enough to play with," said Leonard. "Being a big brother is the best thing ever."

Bubbles Learns to Swim

Bubbles wanted to swim with his friends, but every time he tried, he just kept sinking and blowing big watery bubbles. "I don't like swimming," he said, splashing about in his spotty armbands.

"Swish your arms and kick your legs, like me," said Dad.
But when Bubbles tried, water shot up his nose and into
his ears. "I hate swimming," he spluttered.

Everyone else had a lovely time swimming in the pool.
Alex and Sammy were whizzing down the water slide.
"Come on, Bubbles," they said. "It's great fun."

Bubbles felt very cross. "Swimming is rubbish," he shouted, kicking his legs and swishing his arms, angrily.
Then, suddenly, Bubbles began to move.

"Bubbles, you're swimming!" cried Dad. "Keep going."

Soon, Bubbles was able to swim right across to his friends. "Well done, Bubbles!" they cried.

It wasn't long before Bubbles was having fun on the water slide, too. "Yippee!" he cried, as he went SPLASH into the water. "I love swimming!"

The Shiny Red Shoes

Angelina was very excited. She was going to a party at Pippa the hippo's house. "Do you want to wear your shiny red shoes?" asked Mum. "They'll match your dress."

"No, thank you," said Angelina. "I'm going to wear my blue shoes."

"But you wear your blue shoes every day," said Mum. "The red ones will look much nicer."

"No, thank you," said Angelina.

At Pippa the hippo's house, Angelina waved to her friend, Sarah. She had a lovely yellow party dress on and shiny shoes to match. Angelina looked down at her everyday blue shoes and they looked very scruffy.

Then, Tommy came running over to say hello. He had his best jeans on and lovely new trainers. Angelina looked down at her blue shoes. They didn't look very nice at all.

"I wish I'd worn my shiny red shoes," said Angelina and her lip quivered. Mum gave a big smile and pulled Angelina's shiny red shoes out of her handbag. "I brought them along, just in case you changed your mind," she said.

Angelina was very happy. She quickly put on the shiny red shoes. "Thank you, Mummy," she said. "I love you almost as much as my lovely red shoes."

Then, Angelina ran inside and had a lovely time at Pippa the hippo's party.

Don't Worry, Wanda

Wanda was on the roundabout at the park. Round and round, it whizzed and swished. But Wanda was worried that it would go too fast.

"I feel dizzy," she wailed, "I want to get off."
"Don't worry, Wanda," said Mum. "We'll try the
swings instead."

The little swing swung back and forth. But Wanda was worried that it would go too high. Her little chin quivered and she began to cry.

"My tummy feels funny and I want to get off," she sobbed. "Don't worry, Wanda," said Mum and she took her hand. "We'll try the slide instead."

At the slide, Mum said, "I'll hold your hand. Let's count to three." So, Mum counted one, two, three and *wheee!* Wanda slid all the way to the bottom.

"That was fun!" cried Wanda. "Can I do it again?"
Very soon, Wanda was sliding down all by herself and Mum
was very pleased. "You see, Wanda," she said, "there's really
no need to worry at all."

Franky's Shadow

One night, Franky had a bad dream. So, he got out of bed and crept along the landing to Mum and Dad's room. But something was following Franky.

It was big and grey and had arms and legs. When Franky moved, it moved, too. When Franky stood still, it stood still, too. Franky didn't like the strange shape following him.

"MUMMY!" cried Franky, at the top of his voice.
"There's a monster following me."

Mum and Dad came running out of their room.
"It's not a monster," said Mum. "It's just your shadow."

"My shadow had a bad dream, too," said Franky.
So, Mum and Dad took Franky to snuggle down in
their room. After that, there were no more bad
dreams for Franky or his shadow.

Night, Night, Fred

It was time for bed at Fred's house. "Come on, Fred,"
said Dad. "The sun's asleep and the moon is bright.
It's time to put away your toys and say goodnight."

44

But Fred didn't want to go to bed. He wanted to play with his toys. "No," he said.
"Come on, now," said Dad and he held out his arms.

But Fred took two steps back and he shook his head and his cheeks went red. "No bed," he said.

"Well," sighed Dad. "Let's play a game instead. Let's pretend the toys are tired after the day. But they can't go to sleep until they're put away. Could you help me to tuck them up in the toy box and say goodnight?"

Fred looked at his toys and he looked at Dad. Then he thought for a while and said, "Alright."

Fred picked up his toys and he kissed them goodnight.
Dad closed the lid of the toy box tight. Fred gave a sigh and
he rubbed his eyes. "I'm tired," he said. "Come on," whispered
Dad and he gently picked up Fred and laid him in his bed.

Fred snuggled into his warm, snoozy quilt and his soft, billowy pillow. Dad was very proud. "Well done," he said, "goodnight," and he turned out the light.

Outside, the moon shone bright, but Fred didn't see because he was fast asleep. Night, night, Fred.